To Page McBrier, Susan Hood, Tracy Newman, Karen Jordan,
Eve Catarevas, Carolyn Arden, and Kathleen Kudlinski—thank you.
And to the town of Helen, Georgia—stay enchanted. —S.M.M.

For Penny, my little goblin —J.P.

Text copyright © 2016 by Susan McElroy Montanari
Jacket art and interior illustrations copyright © 2016 by Jake Parker
All rights reserved. Published in the United States by Schwartz & Wade Books,
an imprint of Random House Children's Books, a division of Penguin Random House LLC, New York.
Schwartz & Wade Books and the colophon are trademarks of Penguin Random House LLC.
Visit us on the Web! randomhousekids.com
Educators and librarians, for a variety of teaching tools, visit us at RHTeachersLibrarians.com
Library of Congress Cataloging-in-Publication Data
Montanari, Susan McElroy.
Who's the grossest of them all? / Susan Montanari ; illustrated by Jake Parker.
—First edition.
pages cm
Summary: "A goblin and a troll argue about who is grosser, until a little girl outgrosses them both" —Provided by publisher.
ISBN 978-0-553-51190-1 (hc : alk. paper)—ISBN 978-0-553-51191-8 (glb : alk. paper)—ISBN 978-0-553-51192-5 (ebk)
[1. Characters in literature—Fiction. 2. Humorous stories.] I. Parker, Jake, illustrator.
II. Title. III. Title: Who is the grossest of them all?
PZ7.M763442Wh 2016 [E]—dc23 2015017793
The text of this book is set in Graham.
The illustrations were rendered in ink and colored digitally.
MANUFACTURED IN CHINA
2 4 6 8 10 9 7 5 3 1
First Edition
Random House Children's Books supports the First Amendment and celebrates the right to read.

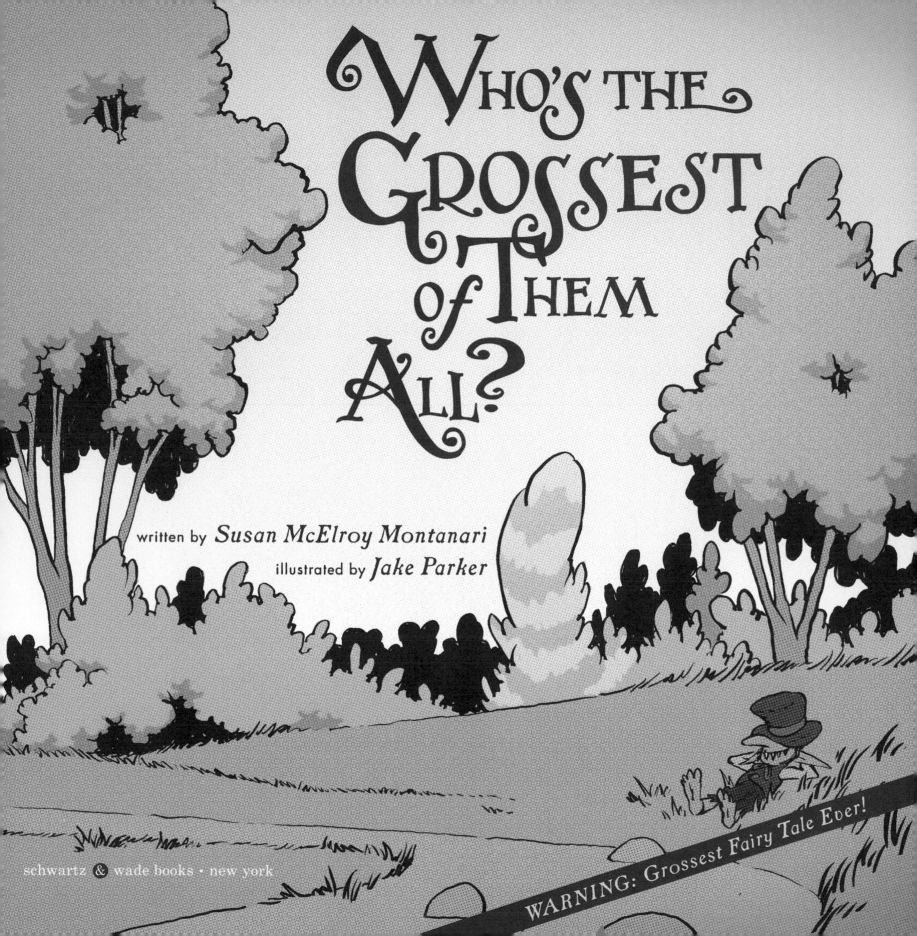

Who's the Grossest of Them All?

written by **Susan McElroy Montanari**

illustrated by **Jake Parker**

schwartz & wade books · new york

WARNING: Grossest Fairy Tale Ever!

"Who's the nastiest, most horrible creature in the forest?" Goblin growled at his reflection. "I am!" he declared, adjusting his hat. "I shall take a stroll through the forest, so that others may appreciate my horribleness."

As Goblin passed a witch's house, she took one look at him and slammed the gingerbread shutters shut. *How rude*, he thought.

A big, bad wolf cowered behind an oak tree. Goblin tipped his hat. The wolf scurried away, his tail tucked between his legs.

Goblin came to a river. Stepping onto the bridge,
he heard a strange grumbling coming from below.

"Who's that tromping on my bridge?!" the grumbly
voice rumbled.

"It is I, Goblin, the nastiest, most horrible creature in
the forest," Goblin answered with a wave of his hand.

"Impossible!" the voice boomed. "*I, Troll*, am
the nastiest, most horrible creature in the forest."

"Ha!" Goblin snorted. "Prove it."

Troll spit on his hands and ran them through his matted hair until the gnarly strands stood straight up. Satisfied, he slithered from beneath the bridge.

"Great gooseberries! You are hideous!" Goblin exclaimed.

"And you're completely grotesque!" Troll marveled. "I've never seen anything like you."

"I have to admit, I can't decide which of us is viler," Goblin said.

"Shall we find someone else to judge?" Troll suggested.

Before long, a man and a goat came clip-clopping by.
"Good sir." Goblin bowed. "Would you be so kind as to
distinguish which of us is the grossest?"

Peeking over the goat's shoulder, the man stuttered, "Y-y-you are both utterly horrifying."

Troll pulled back his blubbery lips. Goblin made sure all one hundred and fifty-two of his glittery teeth were on display. "Choose!" he hissed.

The man pointed at Troll. "S-s-since puke-purple is my least favorite color . . . I would have to say . . . you are the most disgusting."

Troll let out a hoot and did a victory dance. "Thank you!" he shouted as the man and the goat hurried on their way.

"Congratulations." Goblin held out his hand. "You win."

Seeing the wretched look on his rival's face, Troll said, "Aw. Hold on now—that's just one opinion. Perhaps we should get another."

Soon an old woman pushing a wheelbarrow came to the bridge.

"Hello, madam," Troll said, startling her. "If it isn't too much of a bother, could you please discern which of us is the grossest?"

From beneath the wheelbarrow, the woman studied Troll's slimy skin and greasy hair, then turned to Goblin and squinted at his bulbous nose and dangerously sharp teeth.

At last, she said, "You are equally loathsome."

"Arg! What if I do this?" Troll jammed his thumbs in his ears and wiggled his fingers. Then he stuck out his tongue and blew raspberries. Gasping, the woman turned away.

Not to be outdone, Goblin put his hand in his armpit and pumped his arm up and down, producing ghastly sounds.

The woman pointed at Goblin and fled.

"Madam! Madam!" he called after her. "You've left your pumpkins!"

"I don't think she cares," said Troll. "Anyway, that one goes to you. Congratulations."

"Two out of three?" Goblin asked. Troll agreed.

Before long, a small child carrying a basket came to the bridge.

"Try not to scare her," Goblin whispered.

"Right," Troll rumbled. "Excuse me, little girl," he said in his most polite voice.

"I'm not little," said the girl. "I'm big. What do *you* want?"

"We would like to know which of us is the grossest."

The little girl put her finger up her nose.

"Which one of you is grosser?" she repeated, twisting her finger around and around. "Let me think. . . ." She pulled out a big glob of green slime, tapped her chin, then pointed at Troll. "You're totally revolting."

"Thank you," Troll said, leaning away.

The girl's finger circled back to pause precariously close to her mouth. Then she waved it at Goblin. "You're really repulsive, too."

"You're very kind." Goblin shifted sideways.

The girl stared at the two of them, wagging her finger back and forth . . . back and forth . . . until finally she swiped the finger down the front of her dress and said, "The grossest one is . . ."

Goblin and Troll grabbed each other.

"YOU!"

they screamed together.

Troll dove over the side of the bridge, landing—*kerplop!*—in the water, and swam furiously away. As Goblin followed, his hat tumbled from his head and landed near the girl's feet.

The girl shrugged, picked up the hat, and stuck it on her head. "I win!" she declared, and skipped merrily all the way home.

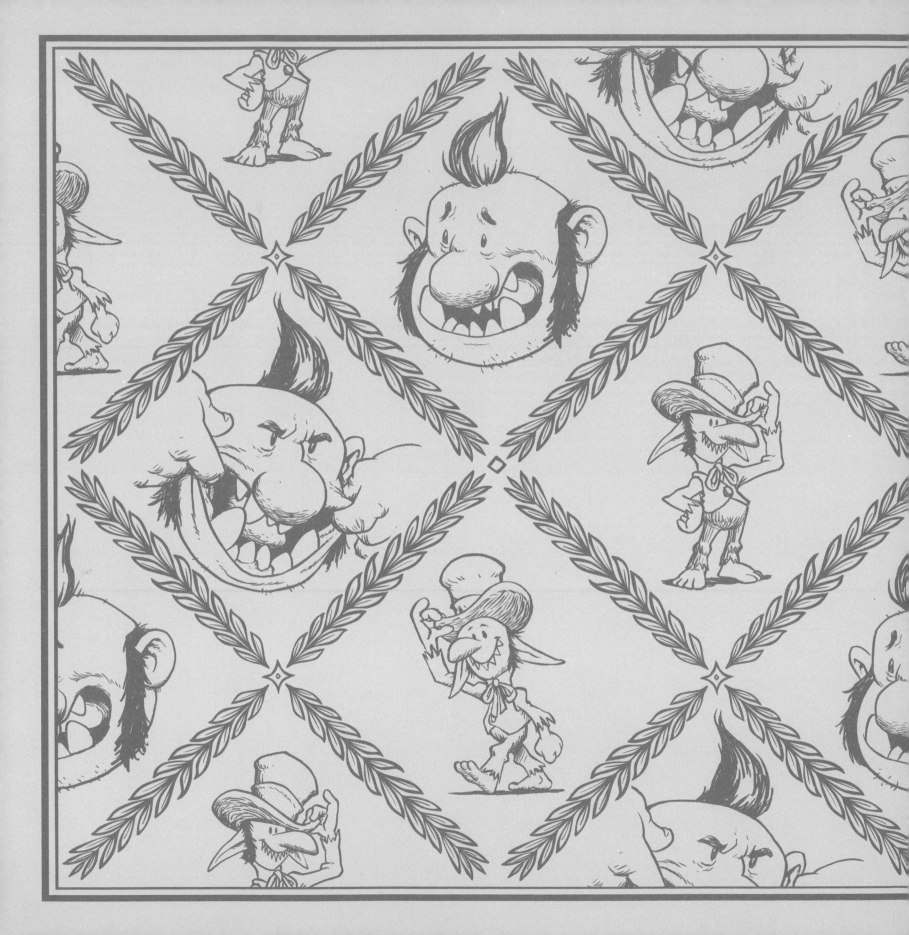